A SUPER FULLBACK FOR THE SUPER BOWL

by CLARE and FRANK GAULT

Pictures by SYD HOFF

SCHOLASTIC INC.

NEW YORK · TORONTO · LONDON · AUCKLAND · SYDNEY · TOKYO

For the young readers
at Wm. Beye School
in Oak Park, Illinois

ISBN 0-590-11904-4

Text copyright © 1977 by Clare S. Gault and Frank M. Gault. Illustrations copyright © 1977 by Syd Hoff. All rights reserved. Published by Scholastic Inc.

14 13 12 11 10 9 8 7 6 5 4   3 4 5 6 7/8

Coach Bronko of the Giants football team was upset.

"Every year it's the same," he said. "My team wins its regular-season games. We get into the Super Bowl. Then we lose. And it's always so close. In the big game, we just can't punch the ball over the goal line.

"Next year it has to be different."

Coach Bronko called his scouts together. "Let's face it, men," he said. "To win the Super Bowl we need a super fullback.

"We have every other player we need — quarterback, pass receivers, line, defense. But we need a super fullback.

"He's got to be big.

"He's got to be tough.

"He's got to run like a tank.

"He's got to get us those tough yards when we need them.

"I want you men to visit every school and college. I want you to look at athletes in every sport. I want you to look everywhere — really beat the bushes. Find us a super fullback."

So the three scouts went looking.

Two months later, the first scout came back. "Coach, I've been to every school. I've been to every college in the country. I've seen plenty of good football players — but I couldn't find a super fullback."

Still later, the second scout came back.

"Coach, I've been to every kind of game. I've looked at every sport — basketball, soccer, track, rowing, weight lifting, ping-pong. I've seen many good athletes — but I didn't find anyone who could be a super fullback."

At last, the third scout came back. His name was Stanley.

"Coach, I've been all over the world. I really beat the bushes as you said. And I found someone — right there in the bushes. He's not exactly what you had in mind, but he might work out."

"Let's see him."

"His name is Og."

"A gorilla? You must be crazy!"

"Look, Coach," Stanley said. "He's big. He's tough. And he runs like a tank. Put a uniform and a helmet on him, and he'll look like any other football player with a beard and a bad temper.

"Believe me, Coach, he's our best hope."

Coach Bronko finally said, "OK, I'll try anything to win the Super Bowl. But you have to train him. And keep him a secret. Not even our own ballplayers can know. We'll use him only if we really need him."

So Stanley trained Og in secret.

First Stanley taught Og how to go into the team's huddle.

He taught Og how to line up for a play.

Then Stanley taught Og how to play fullback:

to run when the ball was snapped . . .

to take the ball from the quarterback . . .

and to keep running until the whistle was
blown.

Stanley taught Og by giving him bananas. Every time Og did the right thing, Stanley gave him a banana. If Og didn't do the right thing, no banana.

After months of practice, Og knew only one play — the fullback plunge, straight ahead.

By that time, the Giants had made it to the Super Bowl. They had won all their games and were champions of their football league. In the Super Bowl they would play the Steelers, champions of the other football league.

On the day of the Super Bowl, Coach Bronko gave a pep talk to his players. "Men, you've got to go out and win," he said. "I know you can do it."

It was a tough game.

First the Giants had the ball. Then the Steelers. Up and down the field they went, but no one was able to score.

Late in the game the score was still 0 to 0.

The Giants had the ball on their own
23-yard line. Time was running out.

Coach Bronko turned to Stanley.
"Go get Og. We have to do something to
move the ball."
The Giants asked for time-out.

Coach Bronko called quarterback Robert Strawback over to the sidelines.

"Strawback," he said, "I'm sending in a new fullback. He may seem a little strange, but don't worry. Just call his play — the fullback plunge."

Og went into the game.

The Giants huddled, then lined up for the next play.

Quarterback Strawback called the signals. He took the ball from the center and handed it off to Og.

There was no hole in the line. But Og plowed through anyway.

Og got to midfield before the Steelers could stop him — a 26-yard gain!

Og went back into the huddle. He held out his hand.

"Ugh, ugh," said Og.

He was waiting for his banana.

Robert Strawback didn't know what Og wanted.

"Great run, fella," he said, and he gave Og's hand a friendly slap.

Og didn't understand.

The Giants lined up for the next play. Strawback handed the ball off to Og. There was no hole in the line, but Og plowed through again. He went all the way to the 16-yard line before the Steelers could stop him — a 35-yard gain!

Og went back into the huddle. This time he held out both hands.

"Ugh, ugh," said Og.

"Fantastic running!" Strawback said, and he slapped both Og's hands.

Og was upset. Where was his banana?

In the huddle, Strawback said, "The Steelers will be waiting for that fullback play again, and they will be ready for it. So, this time we'll change. I'll fake giving the ball to the fullback, then drop back to throw a pass."

Of course, Og didn't know what Strawback was saying.

The ball was snapped. Og ran for the line. But this time Strawback only pretended to give the ball to Og. He kept it himself and dropped back to pass.

Now Og was really mad. First no banana. Now Strawback wouldn't even give him the ball.

Og ran up to Strawback, who was getting ready to throw a pass. He grabbed the ball out of Strawback's hand.

Then Og started to run away with the ball.
The Steelers ran after him.

"Hey, he's running the wrong way!" the
Giants shouted, and they all ran after Og too.

Og ran faster and faster. It seemed as if the whole world was after him.

Og ran across the Giants' goal line and climbed to the top of the goal post.

Just then the gun went off. It was the end of the game. The referee signaled that the Steelers had scored a safety on Og's run.

Og had scored for the wrong team!

The Steelers had won the game, 2 to 0.

Coach Bronko threw his hat on the ground.
"We lost again!" he said. "This is what I get
for monkeying around with a real gorilla."

But Coach Bronko didn't give up. He sent his scouts out again, and at last they came back with a real super fullback for the Giants.

Thanks to the super fullback, the Giants won the Super Bowl the very next year.

And what about Og? What happened to him?

Og stayed with the Giants. They made him
the team's mascot!